Churchill's Cocktails

Churchill's Cocktails

THE CHURCHILL BAR

Published by IWM, Lambeth Road, London SE1 6HZ
iwm.org.uk

© The Trustees of the Imperial War Museum, 2021

Hyatt Regency London – The Churchill
30 Portman Square,
London, W1H 7BH
United Kingdom
Tel +44 (0) 20 7299 2035

ISBN 978-1-912423-39-2

A catalogue record for this book is available from the British Library

Photographs by Hanson Leatherby Photography
Design by Matthew Wilson
Printed and bound in the UK by Gomer Press

All images © IWM unless otherwise stated
Front cover: page 55

Contents

Introduction

If you like a glass of something quite strong mixed with a dash of history, maybe with an added splash of delicious humour, then welcome to a book of cocktail recipes inspired by the colourful and often controversial life of the man voted the 'Greatest Briton' – Winston Churchill.

You will find contained within these cocktail recipes, created by mixologists from The Churchill Bar & Terrace located in Hyatt Regency London – The Churchill, drinks inspired by some of the most famous chapters in the life of Churchill. One famous location synonymous with Churchill, and now part of Imperial War Museums, the Churchill War Rooms, is the historic setting for these cocktails, from where Churchill would eventually 'win the war'.

    The irony of this being a cocktail book based on Churchill's 'finest hours' would not be lost on the man himself. Despite being an enthusiastic drinker of 'Papa's Cocktail', a small amount of scotch mixed in water that was named by his children as they saw him sip it throughout the morning, Churchill himself was no fan of mixed drinks and had an ambivalent attitude to cocktails. It is believed that Churchill may have even 'watered' plants at the White House when visiting President Roosevelt during the war, having accepted one of the president's mixed martinis. Yet it is also undeniable that the pouring away of alcohol was only a temporary and rare event in Churchill's life, for as he famously once said, 'I have taken more out of alcohol than alcohol has taken out of me.'

The amount that Churchill drank daily is, like the man himself, complex and prodigious, but as Churchill himself said when he first began to drink alcohol, he 'learned to like it.' His ability to drink has become one of the many 'myths' that surrounds the man, and one that he never did anything himself to change, believing that the public liked to know their leaders could 'handle' their drink. He even once received a reply from one famous London hotel, after he had queried a bill, that a half-drunk bottle of port he had started was still waiting for him for when he next visited.

One of the ways Churchill avoided the social and practical pitfalls that may come from more excessive drinking was to sip slowly, and so when you make and sample these delicious cocktails this may be an approach to take, as it will allow you to enjoy the unique flavours and tastes that will overflow from these recipes, crafted by expert bar staff from The Churchill Bar. This stylish, must-visit cocktail bar, located in Hyatt Regency London – The Churchill in the heart of Marylebone, is home to an award-winning team of mixologists.

It is no surprise that Churchill was a connoisseur of food and drink and enjoyed large quantities of both. As he sipped scotch and water throughout the day, he would enjoy wine or his favourite drink, Champagne, with meals, followed by a good brandy. But despite this constant drinking, Churchill was to live to the age of 90, write numerous books, paint, develop a hobby as a bricklayer, and lead Britain and her empire to victory during the Second World War. He also once persuaded a doctor to prescribe him a daily dose of alcohol for his recovery after being hit by a car.

Each recipe contained within this book will come with a splash of Churchill history and the recipes have key ingredients that relate to the many stories in Churchill's life. So, if it's a rum cocktail, you can learn about the time Churchill came under fire in Cuba, or a vodka cocktail, when Churchill drank copious toasts with the leader of the Soviet Union, or a whisky cocktail, because he first learned to drink this tipple to help make the water safer whilst serving in the army in India, all are served with a dash of Churchill's famous humour.

As you mix through the recipes contained within these pages, you will find photos of each delicious cocktail at the bar of the Hyatt Regency London – The Churchill in London or in the subterranean world of the Churchill War Rooms. Each cocktail will contain only the finest ingredients, Churchill himself was a fan of certain famous brands, some of which are discussed in the ingredients section of this book. The recipes are divided into difficulty levels, from beginner cocktails such as a simple gin martini to a tequila drink that comes with it's own smoke bubble, reflecting Churchill's love of cigars.

So, sit back, mix, relax and enjoy these cocktail recipes, and remember to savour them during 'Winston Hours' a name given by staff at the White House for the times Churchill visited the U.S. President and they imbibed and enjoyed various drinks and cocktails, all in the name of wartime allied diplomacy.

Churchill, signature cigar in mouth, gives his famous 'V' for victory sign on a visit to Bradford in 1942 (H 25966)

Glossary of Equipment

While many of the cocktails in this book can be made with common kitchen utensils, but for some more specialist mixing equipment may be required. The list below is a brief guide to the equipment the bar staff at The Churchill Bar & Terrace use to create these signature cocktails.

BOSTON SHAKER:
This is a two-piece cocktail shaker, usually consisting of a metal shaker tin and a smaller mixing glass. The larger tin or glass sits snuggly on the smaller vessel to create a sealed shaker.

MIXING GLASS:
A glass or metal container with a spout that is used to chill drinks quickly by stirring with ice rather than shaking the cocktail. The most popular tool for stirred cocktails.

BAR SPOON:
A long-handled spoon used by bar staff to reach the bottom of mixing glasses.

JIGGERS:
Hourglass shaped vessel to measure out a quantity of alcohol, with the smaller 25ml side equivalent to a single shot, and the larger 50ml side a double. Be

aware, they must be filled to the brim to yield the correct alcoholic measure.

MUDDLER:

This is like a pestle, used by bar staff to mash or 'muddle' fruits, spices or herbs in the bottom of a glass. Ideally go for a muddler that measures 15cm to ensure you can reach the bottom of your glass.

FINE STRAINER:

Also often called a mesh strainer, this is used to filter the cocktail into the glass to remove any shards of ice, fruit or fine particles from the final drink.

HAWTHORNE STRAINER:

This strainer has a coil spring which fits into the top of a shaker or mixing glass allowing you to strain from the shaker or mixing glass without letting the ice fall into the serving glass.

SOUS VIDE:

A method of cooking at low temperatures by placing ingredients in plastic pouches. In cocktail recipes this mixes alcohols together without the risk of evaporation, leading to a more delicate flavour. Sous vide machines are widely available.

SMOKING GUN:

An electric, handheld food smoker used mainly in kitchen preparation to quickly finish food with natural smoke. A silicone hose allows you to direct the smoke inside containers, glasses or in the direction you wish.

EMPTY BOTTLE:

A basic and common tool in every bar used to store fresh juices or homemade ingredients. Any empty glass water bottle will do.

Beginner

These simple yet classic cocktail recipes require little pre-preparation, so mix them up and give them a go.

The Churchill Martini

Churchill was said to like a martini served without Vermouth and is often quoted as saying 'glance at the Vermouth bottle briefly, whilst pouring the juniper distillate freely'. This deliciously simple cocktail is a fine introduction to the 'greatest Briton'. You could even have an empty bottle of Noilly Prat Vermouth in your room to feel the true 'spirit' of Churchill whilst enjoying this martini.

INGREDIENTS:
75ml Whitley Neill Gin

GARNISH:
2 Nocellara olives

GLASS:
Corinne Champagne Coupe

EQUIPMENT LIST:
Mixing glass, jigger, bar spoon, Hawthorne strainer

METHOD:
Pour the gin into a mixing glass, add cubed ice and stir for approximately 20 seconds. Double strain into the chilled glass and garnish with the olives, using olive picks if preferred.

The Bitter Truth

Nancy Astor, Britain's first female MP, once allegedly told Churchill, 'If I were your wife I would put poison in your coffee.' Churchill's infamous response, 'Nancy, if I were your husband, I would drink it' has become one of his most famous quips, whether he actually said it or not. The Churchill Bar mixologists have encapsulated this bitter riposte with a cocktail combining rum with Hawaii Kona specialty coffee and a spoon of the herbal bitter Riga Balsam.

....

METHOD:

Brew the coffee. If Hawaii Kona isn't available any specialty coffee with a mild body and bright, fruity aroma can be used. Meanwhile, add the rest of ingredients to a shaker and pour in the coffee once ready. Add cubed ice and shake vigorously. Double strain into the chilled glass. Sprinkle icing sugar around the glass and place the autumn leaf on top of the foam.

INGREDIENTS:

50ml Mount Gay Black Barrel

20ml Mr Black Coffee Liqueur

Spoon of Riga Balsam

Full espresso cup of Hawaii Kona Difference Coffee capsule

15ml sugar syrup

GARNISH:

Autumn leaf (rice paper), icing sugar

GLASS: Gobbler

EQUIPMENT LIST:

Jigger, Boston Shaker, Hawthorne strainer, fine strainer

The Churchill War Rooms Martini

INGREDIENTS:

75ml Inverroche Gin Classic

5 drops Historical War Room Bitters

GARNISH:

1 baby beetroot

GLASS: Nick and Nora

EQUIPMENT LIST:

Mixing glass, jigger, bar spoon, Hawthorne strainer

This truly unique martini has a special ingredient, bitters made from the moisture found within the Churchill War Rooms, the secret wartime bunker in Westminster from where Churchill would lead the nation to victory. However, when making this at home any available bitters will do.

METHOD:

Add the ingredients to a mixing glass, add cubed ice and stir for approximately 20 seconds. Strain into a chilled glass and garnish it with one baby beetroot, on an olive pick if preferred.

The Chartwell

Winston and his wife Clementine enjoyed their time in the gardens of Chartwell, which can now be visited as part of the National Trust. Based on the winter gardens of England, this cocktail combines organic rye vodka with honey and lemon, whilst Greengage Liqueur and homemade basil and ginger juice adds a delightful green hue and zingy finish.

METHOD:

Combine the ingredients in a shaker and dry shake (shake without ice) for 20 seconds, which allows the drink to emulsify and produce a thicker foam on top of the finished drink.

Open the shaker, add cubed ice and shake again vigorously. Double strain into the chilled glass and garnish with the icing ladybird on top of the kaffir lime leaf.

*HOMEMADE COOKING:

Peel the ginger roots, wash properly and juice to get 300ml of liquid. Transfer into a blender, add 90gm of basil leaves and blend for 20 seconds before straining the liquid through a coffee filter paper into the bottle. Refrigerate and consume within five days (mix should produce 30 cocktails).

INGREDIENTS:
30ml Oxford Rye Organic Vodka

25ml Greengage Liqueur

10ml Bergamo Liqueur

25ml honey water

20ml lemon juice

20ml egg white

10ml basil and ginger juice*

GARNISH:
Kaffir lime leaf, icing ladybird

GLASS: Michelangelo Coupette

EQUIPMENT LIST:
Boston Shaker, jigger, bar spoon, Hawthorne strainer, fine strainer

HOMEMADE COOKING INGREDIENTS
300ml fresh ginger juice

90gm basil

HOMEMADE COOKING EQUIPMENT LIST:
Fruit peeler, fruit knife, kitchen scale, juicer or masticating juicer, blender, 350ml empty bottle, coffee filter paper, label

The Aristocratini

This cocktail is crafted with premium Stolichnaya Elit vodka to represent the aristocratic family into which Churchill was born, the Spencer-Churchills. Churchill was born at Blenheim Palace in Oxfordshire, home to the Dukes of Marlborough, and was also a distant relation to Diana, Princess of Wales. Celebrate this aristocratic connection with this deliciously decadent cocktail.

INGREDIENTS:
50ml Stolichnaya Elit vodka

15ml Cocchi Americano

2 dashes Angostura Bitters

GARNISH:
Olive preserved in syrup

GLASS:
Corinne Champagne Coupe

EQUIPMENT LIST:
Mixing glass, jigger, bar spoon, Hawthorne strainer

METHOD:
Add the ingredients to a mixing glass, add cubed ice and stir approximately for 20 seconds. Double strain into the chilled glass and garnish with an olive preserved in syrup.

The Clementine

INGREDIENTS:
30ml Martell Cordon Bleu Cognac

4 dashes Angostura Bitters

Brown sugar cube

Pol Roger Champagne

GARNISH:
Orange peel

GLASS:
Classic Champagne Flute

EQUIPMENT LIST:
Jigger

Winston Churchill proposed to Clementine Hozier in the grounds of Blenheim Palace at the Temple of Diana, and they went on to marry in 1908 at the church of St Margaret in Westminster. To celebrate their 56 years of marriage, this classic Champagne cocktail has a hint of orange in honour of Churchill's beloved Clementine.

METHOD:
Soak the brown sugar cube with 4 dashes of Angostura Bitters. Transfer the cube into the chilled glass, add the cognac and top up the glass with Pol Roger Champagne. Place orange zest on the rim as a garnish.

The Writer

Churchill was a prolific writer, especially of historical and biographical works, winning the Noble Prize for Literature in 1953 and supplementing his modest family income from the numerous books he would write throughout his life. He also wrote film scripts, and to celebrate always finding the sweet spot of any writing, this cocktail is a combination of tangy rhubarb and sweet custard, perfect to curl up with and delve into one of Churchill's many titles.

METHOD:

Combine the ingredients in a Boston Shaker and with a bar spoon mix the jam to dissolve it into the mixture. Dry shake for 20 seconds, which allows the drink to emulsify and produce a thicker foam on top of the finished drink. Open the shaker, add cubed ice and shake again vigorously. Double strain into a chilled glass and garnish the rim with rhubarb powder.

To enjoy this cocktail alcohol free, simply swap the gin for Everleaf Mountain, a complex aperitif similar to pink gin.

INGREDIENTS:
50ml Montagu Gin

45ml William Fox Custard Syrup and yolk mix*

10ml lemon juice

1 teaspoon rhubarb and ginger Jam

20ml egg white

GARNISH:
Rhubarb powder

GLASS: Vintage Coupette

EQUIPMENT LIST:
Boston Shaker, jigger, bar spoon, Hawthorne strainer, fine strainer

*HOMEMADE COOKING:

In a jug combine 350ml of William Fox Custard Syrup and 350ml of egg yolk. Stir the ingredients well and bottle. Refrigerate and consume within three days (mix should produce 15 cocktails).

Churchill makes a radio address at his desk at 10 Downing Street in 1942 (H 20446)

HOMEMADE COOKING INGREDIENTS:
350ml William Fox Custard Syrup

350ml egg yolk

HOMEMADE COOKING EQUIPMENT LIST:
Jug, bar spoon, 700ml empty bottle

2

Intermediate

These cocktails involve a little more preparation including ingredients that can be stored in a fridge before use.

The Enchantress

Churchill greatly enjoyed his time onboard the yacht HMS *Enchantress* when he was First Lord of the Admiralty, once proclaiming it had been his 'greatest toy'. He travelled extensively on the yacht but particularly loved cruising through the Mediterranean, and this cocktail is inspired by his time cruising through the Bay of Naples and Sicily. Inspired by this beautiful and volcanic terrain, this is a unique twist on a classic margarita, a smooth mix with flavours of black lava salt and citrus leaves.

INGREDIENTS:
50ml Dobel Blanco Tequila

15ml star fruit syrup*

20ml lime juice

GARNISH:
Black Lava salt

GLASS: Spiral Glass

EQUIPMENT LIST:
Boston Shaker, jigger, bar spoon, Hawthorne strainer, fine strainer

METHOD:
Add the ingredients to a cocktail shaker, shake with cubed ice and double strain into a chilled glass. Garnished the rim with black lava salt.

*HOMEMADE COOKING:
Using a masticating juicer, juice 200gm of star fruit and strain it through a coffee filter paper into a measuring jug. Add 200gm of white caster sugar and stir the mixture at room temperature to dissolve all the sugar. Strain into a bottle using a coffee filter. Refrigerate and consume within 3 days (mix should produce syrup enough for 13 cocktails).

HOMEMADE COOKING INGREDIENTS:
200gm star fruit

200gm white caster sugar

HOMEMADE COOKING EQUIPMENT LIST:
Masticating juicer, measuring jug, kitchen scale, coffee filter, bar spoon, 500ml empty bottle

The Journalist

INGREDIENTS:
40ml Doble Blanco Tequila

20ml Mastiha Liqueur

10ml lemon juice

2 candy floss grapes

15ml grape syrup*

GARNISH:
Candy floss

GLASS: Crystal Flute

EQUIPMENT LIST:
Boston Shaker, jigger, bar spoon, Hawthorne strainer, fine strainer, muddler

HOMEMADE COOKING INGREDIENTS:
250gm white caster sugar

250ml Champagne (preferably flat)

HOMEMADE COOKING EQUIPMENT LIST:
Cooking pan, measuring jug, kitchen scale, 500ml empty bottle

Churchill started his literary career reporting on wars and conflicts for newspapers and was believed to have a vocabulary of over 65,000 words. President Kennedy famously said that he had 'mobilised the English language'. This cocktail blends tequila with Mastiha Liqueur, lemon juice and is finished with a playful candy floss garnish to represent Churchill's time as a care-free roving journalist.

METHOD:
Add the grapes to a cocktail shaker and muddle them. Combine the rest of the ingredients, shake with cubed ice and double strain into a chilled glass. Garnish with candy floss on the rim.

*HOMEMADE COOKING:
Place pan on a low heat and add 250gm of caster sugar and 250ml of Champagne. Stir gently until it reaches a boiling point. Let the syrup cool down for around 20 minutes and pour into a bottle. Refrigerate and consume within ten days (mix should produce syrup enough for 16 cocktails).

The Prime Minister

Winston Churchill was to finally become Prime Minister in May 1940 aged 65 and at a time of great peril during the Second World War. Faced with tremendous challenges, he united the nation through sheer resilience, wit and unparalleled energy. The Prime Minister cocktail draws inspiration from that classic British food duo of egg and cress. It is a strong cocktail that celebrates simplicity, flair and strength.

INGREDIENTS:
30ml watercress and jasmine cordial*

10ml Bushmills Whiskey

30ml Pedrino Vermouth & Tonic Spritz

1 dash Absinthe

GARNISH:
Pickled beetroot quail egg*

GLASS: Spiral Tumbler

METHOD:
Add all the ingredients except the tonic to a mixing glass, add cubed ice and stir for approximately 20 seconds. Strain over a clear ice cube in a chilled glass and top up with 30ml of tonic. Garnish with pickled beetroot quail egg on an olive pick.

EQUIPMENT LIST:
Mixing glass, jigger, bar spoon, Hawthorne strainer

*HOMEMADE COOKING:
Watercress and jasmine cordial:
Blend 450ml of Muyu Jasmine Liqueur, 50gm of fresh watercress, 8 pea shoots and a pinch of salt until the herbs are completely incorporated into the liquid. Strain with a coffee filter into a bottle. Refrigerate and consume within five days (mix should produce cordial enough for 15 cocktails).

HOMEMADE COOKING INGREDIENTS:

Watercress and jasmine cordial:
450ml Muyu Jasmine Liqueur

50gm fresh watercress

8 fresh pea sprouts

Pickled beetroot quail egg:
Beetroot juice

Jar of cooked and peeled quail eggs

HOMEMADE COOKING EQUIPMENT LIST:
Blender, kitchen scale, coffee filter, measuring jug, jar, knife, wood stick, 500ml empty bottle

Pickled beetroot quail egg:

Strain the liquid from a jar of peeled quail's eggs and fill up the jar 1/3 of white vinegar and 2/3 of beetroot juice. Infuse for 48 hours. Eggs are ready to be cut in half and used as garnish. Refrigerate and consume within one month.

Churchill at Alamein in 1942 (ME RAF 5060)

The Finest Hour

INGREDIENTS:
40ml Chivas Regal 18 Years Old

20ml Carpano Antica Formula Vermouth

20ml Old Engine Oil porter reduction*

2 dashes Angostura Bitters

GARNISH:
Gold Maraschino cherry

GLASS: Michelangelo Coupette

EQUIPMENT LIST:
Mixing glass, jigger, bar spoon, Hawthorne strainer

HOMEMADE COOKING INGREDIENTS:
330ml porter

100gm brown caster sugar

HOMEMADE COOKING EQUIPMENT LIST:
Cooking pan, bottle opener, kitchen scale, measuring jug, bar spoon, 330ml empty bottle

One of Churchill's most famous speeches during the Second World War paid tribute to the 'few' pilots who were to win the Battle of Britain. This cocktail celebrates the RAF's 'finest hour' with a twist on a Manhattan.

METHOD:
Add ingredients to a mixing glass, add cubed ice and stir for approximately 20 seconds. Double strain into a glass, preferable chilled. Garnish with a gold Maraschino cherry.

*HOMEMADE COOKING:
Add bottle of porter and 100gm of brown caster sugar to pan and bring to a simmer. Stir throughout the entire process for approximately 20 minutes. Let the reduction cool down for another 20 minutes and pour it into the bottle. Refrigerate and consume within ten days (mix should produce juice enough for 12 cocktails).

The First Sea Lord

Churchill became First Lord of the Admiralty in 1911 and was to go on and prepare the Royal Navy to fight in the First World War. This cocktail is inspired by Churchill's connection to the Royal Navy, infusing the strong and complex flavour of Pusser's Navy Rum with one of the world best coffees, Jamaican Blue Mountain by Difference Coffee Company. A sweet note of English honey is then added, and the drink is shaken with the smokey and peaty notes of Bowmore 12 Year Old whisky for an incredible finish.

INGREDIENTS:
50ml Jamaican Blue Mountain infused Pusser's Navy Rum*

15ml Bowmore 12 Year Old

15ml honey syrup*

GARNISH:
White chocolate stick

GLASS: Gobbler

EQUIPMENT LIST:
Mixing glass, jigger, bar spoon, Hawthorne strainer

METHOD:
Add the ingredients to a mixing glass, add cubed ice and stir for approximately 20 seconds. Double strain over a clear ice shard in a chilled glass. Garnish with the white chocolate stick on the rim.

*HOMEMADE COOKING:
Honey syrup:
In the pan bring to a simmer 150ml of water and add 150ml of clear honey. Stir gently throughout the entire process until the boiling point is reached. Let the syrup cool down for 20 minutes and pour it into the bottle. Refrigerate and consume within ten days (mix should produce syrup enough for 20 cocktails).

Jamaican Blue Mountain infused Pusser's Navy Rum: Prepare 500ml of rum in measuring jug and grind 25gm of specialty coffee beans with an electric or manual grinder (coffee beans must be ground to medium course like sea salt). Place the ground coffee on top of the V60 brewer and pour the rum on top with the following ratio:

1. First 50ml rum covering all the coffee (this is called blooming process) and after 30 seconds add 100ml of rum in concentric circles above the coffee
2. Let it brew 60 seconds, then add the last 70ml rum
3. Let it all drip (should be done within 3 or 4 minutes. If not, the coffee was grounded too fine)
4. When the brew is finished, place into the 330ml bottle
5. Refrigerate and consume within 10 days (mix should produce rum enough 14 or 15 cocktails)

HOMEMADE COOKING INGREDIENTS:

Honey syrup:
150ml water

150ml clear honey

Jamaican Blue Mountain infused Pusser's Navy Rum:
500ml Pusser's Navy Rum

25ml Jamaican Blue Mountain ground specialty coffee beans

HOMEMADE COOKING EQUIPMENT LIST:

Cooking pan, measuring jug, kitchen scale, bar spoon, 330ml empty bottle

The Iron Curtain

INGREDIENTS:

50ml fennel infused Oxford Rye Organic Vodka*

10ml saffron syrup*

10ml lemon Juice

Three Cents Gentleman Tonic

GARNISH:

White chocolate and strawberry crisp (ready made)

GLASS: Highball

EQUIPMENT LIST:

Jigger, bar spoon

In 1946 Churchill warned in a speech whilst in the United States of an emerging threat from his former ally, the Soviet Union, to the continent of Europe, famously describing an 'Iron Curtain' that had descended there since the Soviet post-war occupation. Many historians now attribute this speech to the start of the Cold War. This vodka-based cocktail is made with some of the finest ingredients to mark this pivotal moment in the 20th century.

METHOD:

Combine the ingredients in the glass, ideally chilled, adding just a splash of tonic. Add a clear ice column and top up the glass with the rest of the tonic water. Garnish with the yellow shard.

To enjoy The Iron Curtain alcohol free, swap the vodka for Everleaf Marine. This retains the delicate drink profile with a lighter body.

*HOMEMADE COOKING:

Fennel infused Oxford Rye Organic Vodka: Combine 100gm of fennel and 700ml of vodka in an airtight container and leave it to infuse at room temperature for 24 hours. Strain the vodka through a coffee filter into the larger bottle, refrigerate and

HOMEMADE COOKING INGREDIENTS:

Fennel infused Oxford Rye Organic Vodka:

100gm fennel

700ml vodka

Saffron syrup:

300ml water

300gm white caster sugar

Half teaspoon of saffron

HOMEMADE COOKING EQUIPMENT LIST:

Cooking pan, pastry paper, airtight container, kitchen scale, measuring jug, bar spoon, 2 coffee filters, 700ml empty bottle, 500ml empty bottle

consume within 1 month (mix should produce infusion enough for 13 cocktails).

Saffron syrup:

Bring 300ml of water to a medium heat in a pan and while stirring slowly add 300gm of white caster sugar (50gm every minute will allow the sugar to better dissolve in the water). Once all the sugar has dissolved, switch off the heat, add a half bar spoon of saffron and let this infuse for 20 minutes. Strain through a coffee filter into the smaller bottle, refrigerate and consume within 10 days (mix should produce syrup enough for 30 cocktails).

Churchill and Roosevelt confer over lunch at the Yalta Conference in February 1945 (EA 52857)

The Empire

This delightful aperitif style cocktail mirrors the type of welcome drinks Churchill served to his guests during his diplomatic days. Churchill was a committed imperialist and first visited another country in the vast British Empire when he arrived in India in 1896 to serve as a soldier.

METHOD:

Add the ingredients to a mixing glass, add cubed ice and stir for approximately 20 seconds. Strain into a chilled glass and garnish with 2 lavender sprigs inside a tailor cut citrus leaf.

*HOMEMADE COOKING:

Citrus mix:

Seal 150ml of grapefruit juice, 150ml of lemon juice, 400gm of white caster sugar, the zest of one whole grapefruit and the peel of three lemons in a vacuum bag and sous vide at 60°C for 60 minutes. Let it cool down for approximately 20 minutes. Strain through the coffee filter into the bottle, refrigerate and consume within ten days (mix should produce enough for 17 cocktails).

INGREDIENTS:
20ml Montagu Hand-crafted Gin

20ml Italicus Bergamot Liqueur

5ml grape syrup

20ml Cocchi Americano aperitif wine

20ml citrus mix*

2 dashes Absinthe

GARNISH:
Tailor cut citrus leaf with 2 lavender sprigs

GLASS: Champagne Flute

EQUIPMENT LIST:
Boston Shaker, jigger, bar spoon, Hawthorne strainer, fine strainer

HOMEMADE COOKING INGREDIENTS:
150ml fresh grapefruit juice

150ml fresh lemon juice

400gm white caster sugar

3 lemon peels

HOMEMADE COOKING EQUIPMENT LIST:
Kitchen scale, measuring jug, fruit peeler, vacuum bag, vacuum sealer, sous vide, coffee filter, 500ml empty bottle

The New Yorker

In 1931, Churchill was seriously injured when he was hit by a taxi while crossing Fifth Avenue in New York. He persuaded the doctors treating him that he should be prescribed alcohol to aid in his recovery from his injuries. This cocktail mixes bourbon whisky which is married with the sweet combination of Elderflower & Gooseberry Gin and Galliano liqueurs, before a few dashes of tomato essence are added to create something truly unique and that would have surely helped Churchill through his difficult recovery.

INGREDIENTS:
30ml Woodinville Bourbon

15ml Elderflower & Gooseberry Gin Liqueur

15ml Galliano

10ml tomato essence*

GLASS: Crystal Tumbler

EQUIPMENT LIST:
Mixing glass, jigger, bar spoon, Hawthorne strainer

METHOD:
Add the ingredients to a mixing glass, add cubed ice and stir for approximately 20 seconds. Double strain over a clear ice chunk into a chilled glass.

*HOMEMADE COOKING:
Cut the tomato in half and with a spoon remove the insides. Place in an airtight container and add 330ml of vodka. Seal the container and leave the tomato to macerate in alcohol for one week. Strain the mixture through a coffee filter into the bottle, refrigerate and consume within one month (mix should produce essence enough for 30 cocktails).

HOMEMADE COOKING INGREDIENTS:
1 tomato

330ml vodka

HOMEMADE COOKING EQUIPMENT LIST:
Fruit knife, spoon, airtight container, coffee filter, 330ml empty bottle

The Charleston Punch

INGREDIENTS:
50ml Botanist Gin

25ml lemon Juice

20ml cloves and pineapple syrup*

40ml soda water

GARNISH:
Dried mini pineapple wheel
(ready made)

GLASS: Crystal Highball

EQUIPMENT LIST:
Boston Shaker, jigger, bar spoon,
Hawthorne strainer, fine strainer

Churchill undertook an extensive tour of the United States and Canada in 1929, mainly for recreation purposes, and visited California where he enjoyed a few nights in the city of San Francisco. This vibrant, cosmopolitan city is reflected in this refreshing cocktail with exotic 'west coast' notes.

METHOD:

Add the ingredients to a cocktail shaker, except the soda, shake with cubed ice and double strain into the chilled glass. Pour the 40ml of soda and add crushed ice. Garnish with the dried pineapple slice.

To enjoy The Charleston Punch alcohol free, simply swap the gin for Seedlip Spice 94. With a slightly lighter body, the notes of Seedlip and the main profile of our homemade pineapple and cloves syrup, make a sophisticated cocktail.

*HOMEMADE COOKING:

Lightly roast 3 cardamon pods, 1 star anise, 3 cinnamon sticks and 25 cloves in a pan. Peel a pineapple, cut into 2cm cubes and add them to the pan, covering everything with 30gm of white caster sugar. Continue to cook at low heat until caramelised. Add 300ml of water and the remaining 300gm

INTERMEDIATE

of white caster sugar and continue stirring at low heat until the sugar has dissolved. Let it cool before straining with a coffee filter into the bottle. Refrigerate and consume within 10 days (mix should produce syrup enough for 15 cocktails).

HOMEMADE COOKING INGREDIENTS:

3 cardamom pods

1 star anise

3 cinnamon sticks

25 cloves

1 pineapple (medium size)

330gm white caster sugar

300ml water

HOMEMADE COOKING EQUIPMENT LIST:

Cooking pan, fruit knife, kitchen scale, bar spoon, 330ml empty bottle, coffee filter

Churchill at the controls of a Boeing 314 flying boat (H 16645)

The V For Victory

On 8 May 1945, millions of people celebrated in the streets to mark the end of the Second World War in Europe. To mark this milestone, a personal triumph for Churchill in the war, this cocktail is features Churchill's favourite Cognac with rhubarb-flavoured liqueur and is balanced with a dry sparkling wine reduction which is infused with kaffir lime leaves. These delightful ingredients are complemented by a few drops of bitters and citric acid for a strong and pleasing finish.

INGREDIENTS:
50ml Remy Martin 1738

20ml Nardini Rabarbaro

2 dashes Angostura Bitters

15ml dry sparkling wine reduction with kaffir lime leaves*

GARNISH: Lemon peel

GLASS: Retro Fizzio Coupete

EQUIPMENT LIST:
Mixing glass, jigger, bar spoon, Hawthorne strainer

METHOD:

Add ingredients to a mixing glass, add cubed ice and stir for approximately 20 seconds. Double strain over a clear ice chunk into a chilled glass. Garnish with a lemon twist on the rim.

*HOMEMADE COOKING:

In the pan bring to a simmer 150ml of sparkling wine, 75ml of water, 4 kaffir lime leaves and add scoop by scoop a total of 250gm of white caster sugar. Once the sugar has dissolved let the mixture cool and add one bar spoon of citric acid. Strain through a coffee filter into the bottle, refrigerate and consume within 10 days (mix should produce reduction enough for 16 cocktails).

HOMEMADE COOKING INGREDIENTS:
150ml sparkling wine

75ml water

4 kaffir lime leaves

250gm white caster sugar

1 bar spoon citric acid powder

HOMEMADE COOKING EQUIPMENT LIST:
Cooking pan, kitchen scale, bar spoon, coffee filter, 330ml empty bottle

INTERMEDIATE

The Gardener

Churchill was often absorbed in a quieter preoccupation whilst at his home in Chartwell, spending time in the butterfly garden. He envisaged "fountains of honey and water", attempted to re-introduce extinct species of butterfly and often hosted famous garden parties in which butterflies played an important part. Containing celery, egg and a duo of peas and carrots, this is a cocktail as fresh as an English garden and a wonderful celebration of Churchill's love of nature.

INGREDIENTS:
45ml Absolut Elyx
25ml celery pea syrup*
25ml acid carrot juice*
20ml egg white

GARNISH:
Dry pea powder

GLASS: Nick and Nora

EQUIPMENT LIST:
Boston Shaker, jigger, Hawthorne strainer, fine strainer

METHOD:

Combine all the ingredients in a Boston Shaker. Dry shake (shake without ice) for 20 seconds, which allows the drink to emulsify and produce a thicker foam on top of the finished drink. Open the shaker, add cubed ice and shake again vigorously. Double strain into a chilled glass and garnish with dry pea powder on top of the foam.

*HOMEMADE COOKING:

Celery pea syrup:
In an pan bring to a boil 400ml of water and add 2 sticks of sliced celery and 40gm of frozen peas. Let it boil for 2 minutes then reduce the heat and slowly add 400gm of white caster sugar until it dissolves into

the water. Let the syrup cool down, strain through a coffee filter into the bottle, refrigerate and consume within 10 days (mix should produce syrup enough for 15 cocktails).

Acid carrot juice:
In a jug combine 300ml of carrot juice and 120ml of supasawa mixer. Bottle, refrigerate and consume within 3 days (mix should produce juice enough for 16 cocktails).

HOMEMADE COOKING INGREDIENTS:

Celery pea syrup:
400ml water

2 celery sticks

40gm frozen peas

400gm white caster sugar

Acid carrot juice:
300ml bottled carrot juice

120ml Supasawa

HOMEMADE COOKING EQUIPMENT LIST:

Cooking pan, kitchen scale, jug, two 500ml empty bottles, coffee filter

3

Advanced

These recipes require more adept mixing skills. Whilst more complex, the end cocktail will have you purring like one of Churchill's favourite wartime cats, Nelson.

The Desert Fox

'May I say, cross the havoc of war, a great general' were the words Churchill used to describe one of the most famous German generals of the war, Erwin Rommel. An admired adversary, Churchill was nonetheless pleased to win the war in North Africa and expel Rommel and his troops from the continent. This gin-based cocktail is finished with elegant notes of chinotto, a fruit that grows on the myrtle-leaved orange tree native to Libya.

INGREDIENTS:
25ml Plymouth Gin Navy Strength
25ml Muyu Chinotto Nero
25ml Campari
Bar spoon of dry lavender

GARNISH:
Lavender smoke

GLASS:
Nude tumbler, served from a bespoke glass bell

EQUIPMENT LIST:
Mixing glass, jigger, bar spoon, smoking gun, Hawthorne strainer

METHOD:
Combine the ingredients in a mixing glass, add cubed ice and stir for approximately 20 seconds. Strain the mixture into a chilled glass over a clear chunk of ice, place the glass inside the glass bell and inject the lavender smoke. Allow the mixture to infuse with the smoke for 5–10 seconds and open the bell to release the smoke.

How to use the smoking gun:
Place a bar spoon of dry lavender in the burn chamber of the smoking gun. Insert the silicone hose of the gun inside the bell and switch on the gun for five seconds. After injecting smoke for five seconds, switch off the machine, take off the silicon hose and close the bell. Always discard the burned material inside the chamber after every use.

The Artist

INGREDIENTS:

60ml Mount Gay Rum XO

25ml Luxardo Sangue Morlacco

25ml maple syrup

25ml pineapple juice

15ml lemon juice

35ml almond milk

1 tea bag

Grated nutmeg, cloves, cinnamon

GLASS: Tea Cup

EQUIPMENT LIST:

Jigger, bar spoon

During Churchill's wilderness years out of politics, he watched his sister-in-law painting and decided to take up the hobby. He went on to create over 550 oil paintings, focusing on landscapes and seascapes. The Artist is a punch-style cocktail, blending notes of traditional milky English breakfast tea with spicy accents of rum and warming cinnamon, also evoking the English countryside in winter in honour of the landscape paintings Churchill enjoyed so much.

METHOD:

Combine all ingredients, except the almond milk, in an airtight container. Take one nutmeg, one clove and one cinnamon stick and grate. Leave the ingredients to infuse together for one hour in the refrigerator. The container should be sealed. Warm up the almond milk in the pan until it reaches a simmer and pour into the container. The almond milk should slightly curdle. Strain the mixture through a coffee filter into the bottle, refrigerate and consume within 5 days.

The Father

Churchill's relationship wth his parents had been difficult and remote, making him determined to do things differently with his own children. Winston and his wife Clementine had five children and he was an affectionate and devoted father. Vowing to spend time with them, Churchill built a tree house at Chartwell, and a summer house for his youngest, Mary. An ode to fatherhood, The Father is a warming, spiced drink inspired by the combination of apple and crumble, celebrating the paternal life of Churchill.

INGREDIENTS:
50ml Boulard Calvados Pays d'Auge

80ml spiced mineral water*

20ml apple sherbet*

10ml Frangelico Liqueur

5ml nutmeg syrup*

GARNISH:
Apple crumble (ready made)

GLASS: Wood Cup

EQUIPMENT LIST:
Jigger

METHOD:

Combine the ingredients in a milk pan or kettle except the liqueur and Calvados. Heat the mixture until you reach the boiling point and transfer into the wooden cup. Add the liqueur and the Calvados, stir and serve with an apple crumble on the side.

*HOMEMADE COOKING:

Spiced mineral water:
Bring to a boil 70ml of water in a pan. The water should include 4 stars anise, 12 cloves, half a tonka bean, a half teaspoon of grated nutmeg and a full teaspoon of grated cinnamon stick. Leave the mixture to simmer for 30 minutes then let it cool. Strain it through a coffee filter into the bottle, refrigerate and

HOMEMADE COOKING INGREDIENTS:

Spiced mineral water:
700ml water

4 star anise

12 cloves

Half a tonka bean

Half teaspoon grated nutmeg

Full teaspoon grated cinnamon stick

Apple Sherbet:
300ml green apple juice

150gm white caster sugar

1 teaspoon citric acid powder

1 teaspoon citric malic powder

Nutmeg syrup:
200ml Water

1 teaspoon grated nutmeg

100gm white caster sugar

HOMEMADE COOKING EQUIPMENT LIST:

Cooking pan and small milk pan, grater, kitchen scale, masticating juicer, bar spoon, 700ml and two 330ml empty bottles, 3 coffee filters

consume within 10 days (mix should produce spiced water enough for 8 cocktails).

Apple sherbet:

With a masticating juicer, squeeze enough fresh green apples to obtain 300ml of apple juice. Mix this with 150gm of white caster sugar, 1 teaspoon of powdered citric acid and 1 teaspoon of powdered citric malic. Once all the ingredients dissolve into the juice, bottle, refrigerate and consume within 5 days (sherbet should be enough for 15 cocktails).

Nutmeg syrup:

In a small pan bring to a boil 200ml of water with 1 teaspoon of grated nutmeg. Let it boil for 2 minutes then reduce the heat and add gently 100gm of white caster sugar. Stir the mixture util the sugar dissolves then let it cool down for approximately 20 minutes. Strain through a coffee filter into the bottle, refrigerate and consume within 10 days (mix should produce syrup enough for 20 cocktails).

The Spitfire

The Spitfire was the RAF's most famous plane in the Second World War, and you can still see them fly today at IWM Duxford. Churchill had been a great advocate of developing modern fighters before the war, and he was repaid when the Spitfire and Hurricane were integral to the RAF's victory in the Battle of Britain in 1940. In honour of this majestic plane, which is synonymous with Churchill himself, this rum based cocktail has green and brown hues to replicate the camouflage found on them.

INGREDIENTS:
40ml Havana Club 7 Years

15ml Cocchi Americano

10ml roasted artichoke syrup*

25ml cold brew coffee

GARNISH:
Dehydrated artichoke*

GLASS: Vintage Old Fashioned

EQUIPMENT LIST:
Boston Shaker, jigger, bar spoon, Hawthorne strainer, fine strainer

METHOD:
Add the ingredients to a mixing glass, add cubed ice and stir for approximately 20 seconds. Strain into a chilled glass over a clear ice cube.

*HOMEMADE COOKING:
Roasted artichoke syrup:
Start the process by preparing a sugar syrup. In a pan warm up 150ml of water, then while stirring add 150gm of white caster sugar (25gm every minute until in order to let the sugar dissolve better into the water). Once all the sugar has dissolved, switch off the heat and let the syrup cool down. Meanwhile, lightly roast in the pan 1 artichoke, cut in half and place in a vacuum bag with the syrup. Seal and sous

HOMEMADE COOKING INGREDIENTS:

Roasted artichoke syrup:
150ml water

150gm white caster sugar

1 small artichoke

Dehydrated artichoke:
1 artichoke

vide for 30 minutes at 60°C. Let the syrup cool down for approximately 20 minutes and strain it through a coffee filter into the 330ml bottle. Refrigerate and consume within 10 days (mix should produce syrup enough for 10 cocktails).

Dehydrated artichoke:
Trim an artichoke and cut in half. Remove the 'hair' and all the tips, slice each half and place them on an oven tray on pastry paper. Put in oven for 7–8 minutes at 180 C°.

HOMEMADE COOKING EQUIPMENT LIST:
Cooking pan, Kitchen scale, measuring jug, bar spoon, oven, pastry paper, fruit knife, v60 coffee maker, kettle, 3 coffee filters, two 330ml empty bottles

The Lover

INGREDIENTS:
40ml Ketel One Vodka

15ml nutmeg syrup*

10ml double cream

3 bar spoon strawberry chutney*

GARNISH:
Whipped cream and
strawberry crisp

GLASS: Champagne Glass

EQUIPMENT LIST:
Jigger, Boston Shaker, bar spoon,
Hawthorne strainer, fine strainer

Winston Churchill was a man who loved his wife Clementine beyond words. A devout family man, a lover of words and the finer things in life, Churchill declared that marrying this clever, formidable, complex woman had been his most brilliant achievement. A celebration of love, loyalty and respect, this cocktail is 'amour' in a glass, a sweet mix of blended strawberries and cream with a whisper of nutmeg.

METHOD:
Combine all the ingredients in the shaker and with a bar spoon mix the chutney to dissolve it into the mixture. Add cubed ice and shake vigorously. Double strain into a chilled glass and top with whipped cream and strawberry crisp.

To enjoy The Lover alcohol free, simply swap the Ketel One Vodka with Everleaf Mountain. The complexity of the chutney and sweet ingredients gives this cocktail the feeling of a dessert.

*HOMEMADE COOKING:
Strawberry chutney:

In a jug muddle 900gm of fresh strawberries and add 2 sliced green chillies, 15ml of fresh lemon juice,

2 tablespoons of chilli flakes, 3 cardamon pods and half a tablespoon of grated nutmeg. Place the mixture in a pan on a low heat and stir until it becomes very thick. Let the chutney cool down for approximately 20 minutes then transfer to the jar. Refrigerate and consume within 3 days (should produce chutney enough for 15 cocktails).

Nutmeg syrup:
In a small pan bring to a boil 200ml of water mixed with 1 teaspoon of grated nutmeg. Let it boil for 2 minutes, reduce the heat and slowly add 100gm of white caster sugar. Stir the mixture util the sugar dissolves then let it cool down for approximately 20 minutes. Strain through a coffee filter into the bottle, refrigerate and consume within 10 days (mix should produce syrup enough for 20 cocktails).

HOMEMADE COOKING INGREDIENTS:

Strawberry chutney:
900gm fresh strawberries

2 sliced chillies

15ml fresh lemon juice

2 tablespoons chilli flakes

3 cardamom pods

Half tablespoon of grated nutmeg

Nutmeg syrup:
200ml water

1 teaspoon grated nutmeg

100gm white caster sugar

HOMEMADE COOKING EQUIPMENT LIST:

Jug, empty jar, cooking pan, kitchen scale, bar spoon, fruit knife, grater, 330ml empty bottle

Baptism of Fire

Winston Churchill first travelled to Cuba in 1895, where he observed the fighting in the Cuban War of Independence. He came under gun fire for the first time whilst in Cuba, so to commemorate this 'baptism of fire', this cocktail is based on one of Cuba's best rums, Havana Club Selección de Maestros. Havana's rum is mixed with fresh fruit juice including guava and lime and finished with Churchill's favorite LBV Port and Angostura Bitters.

INGREDIENTS:

35ml Havana Club Selección de Maestros

50ml banana chilli shrub*

25ml guava juice

20ml lime juice

20ml LBV Port

2 dashes Angostura Bitters

GARNISH:

Mint, gold dried lime*, banana leaf and cedar wood sheet

GLASS: Crystal Highball

EQUIPMENT LIST:

Boston Shaker, jigger, Hawthorne strainer, fine strainer

METHOD:

Add the ingredients to a cocktail shaker, shake with cubed ice and double strain into a chilled crystal highball glass which has been wrapped in a banana leaf and cedar wood sheet. Garnish with mint and a gold dried lime on top of the chilled glass.

*HOMEMADE COOKING:

Banana chilli shrub:
In a small cup add 90ml of dark rum, muddle in 2 slices of red chilli and leave it to infuse for one hour. In a pan lightly roast ten cloves, two cardamom pods and two cinnamon sticks. Add 150ml of clear honey, 150ml white vinegar, 2 sliced ripe bananas and 4 lime peels. Leave the mixture to simmer at low heat for 20 minutes. Let it cool down for another

20 minutes and strain through a coffee filter into the measuring jug. Add 200ml of fresh lime juice, 150ml orgeat syrup and the rum which is now ready after the infusion with chilli. Strain all the mixture through a coffee filter into the bottle, refrigerate and consume within 10 days (mix should produce shrub enough for 13 cocktails).

HOMEMADE COOKING INGREDIENTS:

Banana chilli shrub:
90ml dark rum

2 slices red chilli

10 cloves

2 cardamom pods

2 cinnamon sticks

150ml clear honey

150ml white vinegar

2 sliced ripe bananas

4 lime peels

Gold dried lime:
Black dried limes (ready-made)

Gold pastry spray

HOMEMADE COOKING EQUIPMENT LIST:

Espresso cup, measuring jug, pan, fruit peeler, bar spoon, fruit knife, coffee filter, 700ml empty bottle

Papa's Cocktail

INGREDIENTS:

50ml Butter and cocoa nibs washed Rebel Yell Bourbon* (700ml for the pre-batched)

20ml Martini Rosso Riserva Rubino (280ml for the pre-batched)

20ml Benedictine Liqueur (280ml for the pre-batched)

2 dashes Aztech and Peychaud Bitters (28 dashes for the pre-batched)

American Oak Barrel (3 litres maximum capacity)

GARNISH: Orange zest

GLASS: Michelangelo Coupette

EQUIPMENT LIST:

Mixing glass, jigger, bar spoon, Hawthorne strainer

Churchill first started to drink whisky whilst serving as a soldier in India. He would often sip whisky and water throughout the day, so much so that his children referred to it as 'Papa's cocktail'. In honour of his favourite tipple, this cocktail marries Rebel Yell bourbon with smooth Rubino vermouth to create a cocktail you could sip all day long.

METHOD:

Pour 90ml of mixture from the barrel into a mixing glass, add cubed ice and stir for approximately 20 seconds. Double strain into a chilled glass and garnish it with an orange zest.

*HOMEMADE COOKING:

Butter and cocoa nibs washed bourbon whiskey: In a pan melt 60gm of unsalted butter and 20gm of cocoa nibs and leave to infuse on low heat for 5 minutes. Place in an airtight container then combine 700ml of the whisky and let it sit at room temperature for an hour. Close the container and place it in the freezer overnight. Once a frozen layer of butter has formed at the bottom of the container, strain the liquid mixture through a coffee filter into the bottle,

HOMEMADE COOKING INGREDIENTS:

60gm unsalted butter

20gm cocoa nibs

700ml bourbon whisky

HOMEMADE COOKING EQUIPMENT LIST:

Cooking pan, measuring jug, kitchen scale, airtight container, coffee filter, 700ml empty bottle

refrigerate and consume within 1 month (mix should produce enough for 13 cocktails).

Instruction for pre-batched (14 serves)

Oxidation and extraction are the two elements that will affect the drink depending from how long you leave the liquid in the barrel.

Once the homemade ingredients are bottled, using a funnel, pour all the quantity for the pre-batched in the barrel and leave the mixture to age for approximately 14 days.

The 'Pink' Hush-Hush

Known for his smart suits and style, less well known is that Britain's wartime leader was a fan of wearing pale pink silk underwear. When Winston Churchill claimed the soft texture of woven silk underwear was vital to his well-being, he said 'I have a very delicate and sensitive cuticle which demands the finest covering.' In honour of his under-garment choices, this delicious pink cocktail is as silky as a pair of, well, Churchill's silk underwear, just keep 'hush hush' about it.

INGREDIENTS:
30ml pink peppercorn infused Cocchi Americano*

30ml Luxardo Bianco

40ml Pedrino Ruby Port & Tonic

GARNISH: Pink coaster

GLASS: Vintage Old Fashioned Tumbler

EQUIPMENT LIST:
Jigger, mixing glass, bar spoon

METHOD:

Pour the ingredients into a mixing glass except the tonic. Add cubed ice and stir for approximately 20 seconds. Pour the mixture into a chilled glass and top up with the 40ml of tonic. Serve over large chunk of ice.

*HOMEMADE COOKING:

Pink peppercorn infused Cocchi Americano vermouth:

Seal 100gm of pink peppercorn with 500ml of vermouth and sous vide at 50°C for 30 minutes. Let the infusion cool down for approximately 20 minutes, strain through a coffee filter into the bottle. Refrigerated and consume within 1 month (infusion will be enough for 13 cocktails).

HOMEMADE COOKING INGREDIENTS:
100gm pink peppercorn

500ml Cocchi Americano vermouth

HOMEMADE COOKING EQUIPMENT LIST:
Vacuum bags, vacuum sealer, sous vide, kitchen scale, coffee filter, 500ml empty bottle

The Correspondent

INGREDIENTS:
40ml toasted bread infused
Havana Club 3 Years*

30ml fortified butter syrup*

40ml Veuve Cliquot Brut

GARNISH:
Chocolate bread (ready-made)

GLASS: Tumbler

EQUIPMENT LIST:
Mixing glass, jigger, bar spoon,
Hawthorne strainer

Winston Churchill was often in his early life reporting on wars from around the world. He was captured whilst being a correspondent during the Boer War, later escaping which led to his worldwide fame. This refreshing yet firm cocktail is to honour Churchill's escape from captivity, and features toast and butter, in homage of the meagre rations Churchill had whilst fleeing from his captors.

METHOD:
Combine the ingredients in a mixing glass, except the champagne. Add cubed ice and stir for approximately 20 seconds. Strain over a clear ice column in a chilled glass and top it up with 40ml of champagne. Garnish with two chocolate bread cookies on the side.

*HOMEMADE COOKING:
Toasted bread infused Havana Club 3 Years:
Toast three slices of bread and seal them with 700ml of white rum in a vacuum bag. Sous vide at 50°C for 30 minutes. Let the infusion cool down for approximately 20 minutes and strain through a coffee filter into the bottle. Refrigerate and consume within 1 month (mix should produce infusion enough for 14 cocktails).

Fortified butter syrup:
In a pan melt 100gm of salted butter and let it cool. Transfer to an airtight container, combine with 500ml of Cachaça and place in the freezer overnight. Once a frozen layer of butter has formed at the bottom of the container, strain the liquid mixture through a coffee filter into a measuring jug. Add 1 litre of sugar syrup, stir to combine and pour into a bottle. Refrigerate and consume within 10 days (mix should produce syrup enough for 14 cocktails).

HOMEMADE COOKING INGREDIENTS:

Toasted bread infused Havana Club 3 Years:
700ml Havana Club 3 Years
3 toast slices

Fortified butter syrup:
100gm salted butter
500ml Cachaça
1 litre of sugar syrup

HOMEMADE COOKING EQUIPMENT LIST:

Kitchen scale, measuring jug, toaster, vacuum bags, vacuum sealer, sous vide, cooking pan, airtight container, bar spoon, airtight container, 2 coffee filter, two 700ml empty bottles

Experienced

Unleash your inner bartender and try these cocktails, for as Churchill would surely agree, master these and it will really be your 'finest hour'.

The Bon Vivant

Churchill was a legendary 'bon vivant' and a lover of the finer things in life, from Cuban cigars to whisky and fine dining. He was known to love a consommé before bed and sipped a whisky and soda throughout the day, so in honour this creamy and slightly sweet 'Bon Vivant' cocktail draws inspiration from scones and clotted cream and is testament to his exquisite tastes and a life well lived.

INGREDIENTS:

50ml American Eagle 12 Years Old Bourbon

10ml Cocchi Americano

15ml dry sherry reduction*

6 dashes scone extract*

Spray of raisins essence*

GLASS:

Crystal Glass and Decanter

EQUIPMENT LIST:

Mixing glass, jigger, bar spoon, Hawthorne strainer

METHOD:

Combine the ingredients to a mixing glass, add cubed ice and stir for approximately 20 seconds. Strain the ingredients into a spirit decanter and keep refrigerated until you want to consume your cocktail. Strain the liquid in the spirit decanter in the glass over a clear ice cube. Spray the essence over the drink to finish.

*HOMEMADE COOKING:

Dry sherry reduction:

In a pan bring to a simmer 400ml of dry sherry, let it simmer for 5 minutes. Reduce the heat and add 120gm of white caster sugar. Let the reduction cool down for approximately 20 minutes, bottle it, refrigerate, and consume within 1 month (mix should produce reduction enough for 13 cocktails).

Scone extract:

Seal in a vacuum bag one half scone and 200ml of vodka. Sous vide at 50°C for 30 minutes and let cool for approximately 20 minutes. Place the bag in the freezer for 24 hours and once all the sediments freeze at the bottom of the bag, strain through a coffee filter into a bottle. Refrigerate and consume within 1 month (mix should produce extraction enough for 40 cocktails).

Raisins essence:

Seal in a vacuum bag 150ml of vodka and 15gm of raisins. Sous vide at 50°C for 30 minutes and let cool for approximately 20 minutes. Strain the essence through a coffee filter into a bottle, refrigerate and consume within 1 month (mix should produce essence enough for 30 cocktails).

HOMEMADE COOKING INGREDIENTS:

Dry sherry reduction:
400ml dry sherry

120gm white caster sugar

Scone extract:
200ml vodka

1 half scone

Raisins essence:
140ml vodka

15gm raisins

HOMEMADE COOKING EQUIPMENT LIST:

Kitchen scale, cooking pan, measuring jug, bar spoon, airtight container, 2 vacuum bags, vacuum sealer, sous vide, 3 coffee filter, 500ml empty bottle, two 330ml empty bottles, empty spray bottle of 200ml

The Cigar Smoker

INGREDIENTS:

50ml green pepper infused
Dobel Diamante Tequila

20ml grapefruit oleo saccharum*

30ml tomato shrub*

30ml salted cacao husk brew*

30ml Noilly Prat

GARNISH:

Salt and vinegar powder with
smoke bubble

GLASS: Martini

EQUIPMENT LIST:

Mixing glass, jigger, bar spoon,
Hawthorne strainer

Winston Churchill's most well-known feature was probably a cigar held between his teeth. His love for cigars began when he travelled to Cuba, his preferred brand being Romeo y Julieta. Drawing inspiration from the British staple of salt and vinegar, The Cigar Smoker cocktail promises a touch of theatre by using an aromatic 'smoke bubble' to represent Churchill's cherished love for his cigars.

METHOD:

Combine the ingredients in a mixing glass, add cubed ice and stir for approximately 20 seconds. Strain into a chilled glass pre-garnished with salt and vinegar powder on the rim. With the use of a JetChill Flavour Bluster gun, garnish the top of the drink with a smoked bubble.

*HOMEMADE COOKING:

Green pepper infused Dobel Diamante Tequila:
Slice a whole green pepper, remove the seeds and place in the oven. Cook it at 200°C for 15 minutes. Once the pepper slices are ready, seal with 700ml of tequila and sous vide at 50° for 30 minutes. Let the infusion cool for approximately 20 minutes and strain through a coffee filter into the bottle. Refrigerate and consume within 1 month (mix should produce infusion enough for 13 cocktails).

HOMEMADE COOKING INGREDIENTS:

Green pepper infused Dobel Diamante Tequila:
1 green pepper
700ml tequila blanco

Grapefruit oleo saccharum:
2 grapefruit peels
1 lemon peel
2 kaffir lime leaves
300gm white caster sugar
50ml grapefruit juice

Tomato shrub:
150ml of juice from a large beef tomato
75ml white vinegar
65ml clear honey
65ml water
2 ginger slices
1 cinnamon stick
1 tablespoon of smoked paprika

Salted cacao husk brew:
12gm organic cacao husk
600ml water

HOMEMADE COOKING EQUIPMENT LIST:

Kitchen scale, fruit knife, oven, bar spoon, vacuum bags, sous vide, fruit peeler, lemon squeezer, pan, 4 coffee filters, empty jam jar, two 700ml empty bottles and one 500ml empty bottle

Grapefruit oleo saccharum:
Seal the peels from 2 grapefruits and 1 lemon, 2 kaffir lime leaves, 300gm of white caster sugar, 50ml of grapefruit juice and sous vide at 50°C for 1 hour. Let the mixture cool for approximately 20 minutes and strain through a coffee filter into a bottle. Refrigerate and consume within 1 month (mix should produce oleo enough for 15 cocktails).

Tomato shrub:
Juice with a masticating juicer one large beef tomato in order to get 150ml of tomato juice. In a saucepan lightly roast 2 ginger slices, 1 cinnamon stick, 1 tablespoon of smoked paprika and add the 150ml of tomato juice. Add to the mixture 75ml of white vinegar, 65ml of clear honey, 65ml of water and cook for 15 minutes over a low heat. Allow the shrub to cool down for approximately 20 minutes and strain it through a coffee filter. Store it in a jam jar, refrigerate and consume within 1 month (mix should produce shrub enough for 13 cocktails).

Salted cacao husk brew:
In the pan bring 600ml of water to the boil, then add 12gm of organic cacao husk and a bar spoon or extra fine salt. Brew for 2 minutes then strain through a coffee filter into the bottle. Allow the mixture to cool down for approximately 20 minutes then bottle, refrigerate, and consume within 3 days (mix should produce brew enough for 20 cocktails).

The Traveller

In an era when air travel was cumbersome and uncomfortable, Churchill travelled farther and more extensively than any other wartime leader, being a strong believer in face-to-face negotiations with his counterparts. As Prime Minister during the war he made at least 25 trips outside Britain, spanning the continents. The Traveller cocktail is a nod to the ultimate nostalgia-laden, British homemade comfort food, jacket potatoes and beans, garnished with a dry mashed potato shard and a single baked bean.

INGREDIENTS:
60ml baked potato infused Vestal Vodka*

20ml pinto beans orgeat*

20ml Muyu Chinotto Nero

30ml acid pandan leaf soda*

GARNISH:
Dry potato shard* with baked bean on top

GLASS: Nude Highball Mirage

EQUIPMENT LIST:
Mixing glass, jigger, bar spoon, Hawthorne strainer

METHOD:

Combine the ingredients in a mixing glass, except the soda. Add cubed ice and stir for approximately 20 seconds. Double strain over clear ice in a chilled glass and top up with 30ml of the soda. Garnish with a potato shard on top of the glass and a baked bean.

*HOMEMADE COOKING:

Baked potato infused Vestal Vodka:
Peel and wash three medium red potatoes then slice them. Transfer them to a baking tray and bake in the oven for 25 minutes at 190°C. Let cool and seal the baked potatoes in an vacuum bag with 700ml of vodka. Sous vide for 30 minutes at 50°C and again let cool. Strain through a coffee filter into a bottle,

HOMEMADE COOKING INGREDIENTS:

Baked potato infused
Vestal Vodka:
700ml vodka

3 red potatoes

Pinto beans orgeat:
120gm pinto beans

300ml water

200gm white caster sugar

Acid pandan leaf soda:
500ml water

2 pandan leaves

1 teaspoon citric acid powder

Dry potato shard:
4 Désirée potatoes

Bottle of mineral water

HOMEMADE COOKING EQUIPMENT LIST:

Kitchen scale, knife, oven, blender, pastry paper, measuring jug, kitchen scale, sous vide, vacuum bag, 3 coffee filters, two 700ml empty bottles, hand blender, baking tray

refrigerate and consume within 1 month (mix should produce infusion enough for 13 cocktails).

Pinto beans orgeat:
In a jug soak 120gm of pinto beans in water for 4 hours. Replace the water, wash the beans and transfer to a blender with 300ml of water and blend until you make a paste. Double strain the mixture with a fine strainer and add to a pan with 200gm of sugar. Cook over a low heat for 15 minutes. Strain through a coffee filter into a bottle, refrigerate and consume within 5 days (mix should produce orgeat enough for 15 cocktails).

Acid pandan leaf soda:
In a pan bring to a simmer 500ml of water and 2 pandan leaves for about 15 minutes. Let the mixture cool for approximately 20 minutes and strain through a coffee filter into a measuring jug. Add a teaspoon of citric acid, stir gently until the powder dissolves then transfer the mixture to the CO_2 Syphon (1/2 litre size). Charge the syphon twice with the CO_2 chargers and the soda is ready. Refrigerate and consume within 3 days (mix should produce soda enough for 16 cocktails).

Dry potato shard:
Peel and wash 4 Désirée potatoes, slice them thinly and bake in the oven with steam function for 15 minutes at 140°C. While the potatoes are still hot, blend them with a hand blender while slowly adding mineral water to create a puree that is smooth and thick. Transfer the puree to a baking tray and spread thinly to cover. Bake in the oven at 110°C for 20 minutes until completely dry and crispy. Brake the surface creating potato shards of the size that you like. Store on an dry place and consume within 10 days. (Should produce garnishes enough for 15 cocktails.)

Glossary of homemade ingredients

ACIDS:

Commonly refers to citric, malic and tartaric acid and they are used as replacement for citrus fruit in cocktail.

BREWING:

It is a technique that you use to prepare hot beverages. The classic example is the traditional tea made by brewing tea leaves in a bag in hot water.

BARREL AGING COCKTAIL:

This is the perfect way to give to your cocktail depth, complexity and notes of the barrel flavour. In order to reach the correct flavour profile, you must avoid fresh ingredients such as fruits, citrus ingredients while instead the perfect options are always spirits, liqueurs and bitters. In fact, the best cocktails to age, are classics like Negroni, Manhattan, Sazerac, Boulevardier.

Oxidation and extraction are the two element that will affect the liquid depending from how long you leave it into the barrel.

CHUTNEY:

Like jams and pickles it is a wonderful preserve. A chutney is made with fruit, vegetables or a mix of both. Slow cooked with spices, herbs, vinegar, sugar and usually left in the pot to mature.

CORDIALS:
Sweet liqueurs flavored with fruits, herbs, botanicals or spices. Most of them are under 35% alcohol.

ESSENCE/EXTRACT:
Technique consisting in placing an raw material into alcohol. This is extracting the elements from the raw material into the liquid. With essence, we tend to refer to a 'culinary strength' like our tomato essence but it is just another term for extract and flavoring.

FAT WASH:
It is an technique of flavoring a spirit with any fatty food ingredients such as butter, cheese, oil, fish meat. The mixture is then frozen and the fat is separate due to different freezing points.

INFUSION:
Soaking fruits, herbs, spices or whatever you want to extract the flavor from in liqueur and then strain it off. The higher the proof of the liqueur/spirit, the more flavour it will extract.

MILK PUNCH:
In the past was one of the first drink which was prepared with the clarified milk technique. This method involves the use of an acidic ingredients (usually lemon juice) to curdle the milk, separating it into curds and whey. Once filtered, the result will be an a clear liquid with an lot of complexity.

OLEO SACCHARUM:
From the Latin 'oil-sugar' it is the name given to a sort of syrup made by extracting the natural oils in citrus fruit peels.

REDUCTION:

Refers to a technique that delivers intensely flavored liquid just by simmering or boiling the mixture till we reach the desired concentration. This process is reached by evaporation, consequentially any alcoholic ingredients processed with this technique will lose part of their ethanol decreasing the ABV.

SHERBET/SHRUB:

In our homemade recipes, a shrub involves replacing the acidic ingredients with vinegar.

SODA:

Otherwise known as fizzy water. Can be easily made at home using a soda stream.

SYRUP:

It is an thick, sweet liquid made by dissolving sugar into water. Usually it tend to be made following two basic criteria:

'One part of sugar and one part of water (1:1)' *or*

'two part of sugar and one part of water (2:1)'.

Churchill and his wife Clementine on the Thames, viewing bomb damage to the docks, in 1940 (H 4366)

Acknowledgements

Thanks go to Konstantinos Karampelias, Daniele Bresciani and all of the staff at the Churchill Bar for creating such delicious cocktail recipes, as well as Caroline Major, Olga Mudryakova, Victoria Osman and many others from the Hyatt Regency London – The Churchill for all of their efforts behind the scenes to help make this book happen.

Also to Kieran Whitworth for providing unrivalled Churchill knowledge throughout, to Hanson and Jeni Leatherby for the incredible photography and staging of the 30 cocktails, Matthew Wilson for his keen eye for design and the team at Gomer Press for producing such a beautiful book. Many thanks as well to the team at IWM Publishing.